I SPY

A PENGUIN

For Hartman, Hirshey,
Mansfield, McGuirk, & Stokes
—J.M.

For Oscar Mindich
—W.W.

Text copyright © 2005 by Jean Marzollo.
"Flight of Fancy" and "Sweet Dreams" from *I Spy Fantasy* © 1994 by Walter Wick; "Blocks" and "Cubbies" from *I Spy* © 1992 by Walter Wick; "The Birthday Hunt," "The Hidden Clue," and "The Secret Note" from *I Spy Mystery* © 1993 by Walter Wick; "Peanuts and Popcorn" from *I Spy Fun House* © 1993 by Walter Wick; "The Library" from *I Spy Spooky Night* © 1996 by Walter Wick; "Sorting and Classifying" from *I Spy School Days* © 1995 by Walter Wick

Library of Congress Cataloging-in-Publication Data is available.

ISBN-13: 978-0-439-73862-0
ISBN-10: 0-439-73862-8

30 29 28 27 26 25 24 23 22 21 20   10

Printed in the U.S.A. 40 • This edition first printing, May 2008

BEGINNING READER
LEVEL 1
50-250 WORDS

I SPY
A PENGUIN

Riddles by Jean Marzollo
Photographs by Walter Wick

Cartwheel
·B·O·O·K·S·®

SCHOLASTIC INC.
New York Toronto London Auckland Sydney
Mexico City New Delhi Hong Kong Buenos Aires

I spy

 red lips,

two rings,

 an ax,

a turtle,

 a ship,

and three silver jacks.

I spy

two trucks,

 a penguin,

a pig,

 a horse lying down,

and a number
that's big.

I spy

a ballerina,

 a bow,

a striped cat,

 an ice-cream treat,

and a small straw hat.

I spy

 a seashell,

a dog,

 five stars,

a colorful plane,

and two old cars.

I spy

a trunk,

 two antlers,

a die,

a zebra,

 a basket,

and a lonely eye.

I spy

a panda,

 a purple unicorn,

a lunch box,

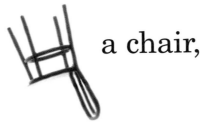 a chair,

and an ear of corn.

I spy

a clown,

 a cat,

 an O,

a castle pin,

 and a yellow bow.

I spy

a cactus,

 four bowling pins,

a pretty black shell,

 and yellow fish fins.

I spy

an anteater,

 a tasty hot dog,

a compass,

 a lock,

and a spotted frog.

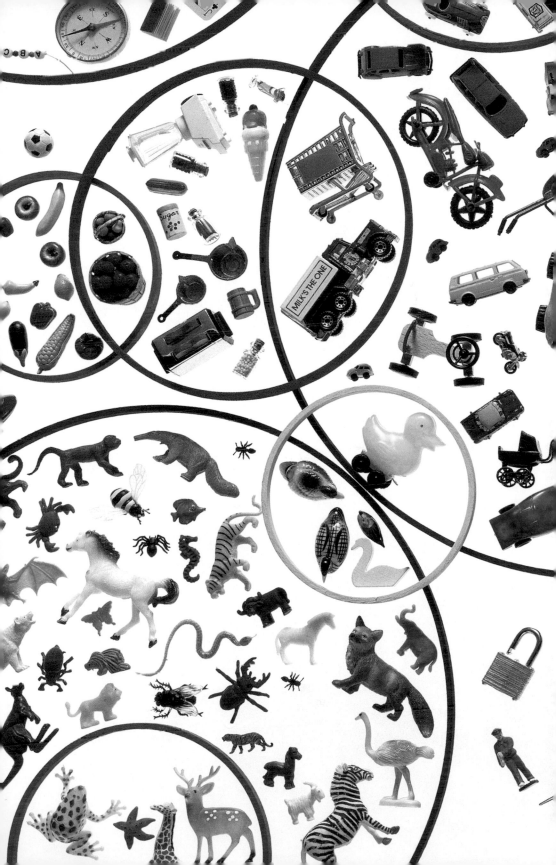

I spy

 a puppy's tongue,

 a bat,

 a V,

 a little blue car,

 an N,

 and a C.

I spy two matching words.

yellow bow

 yellow fish fins

spotted frog

I spy two matching words.

dog

 red lips

tasty hot dog

I spy two words that start with the letter L.

horse lying down

 striped cat

 lonely eye

I spy two words that start with the letters STR.

 striped cat

ballerina

small straw hat

I spy two words that end with the letter N.

penguin

ice-cream treat

clown costume

I spy two words that end with the letters CKS.

three silver jacks

ear of corn

two trucks

I spy two words that rhyme.

 dog

zebra

 frog

I spy two words that rhyme.

five stars

two old cars

purple unicorn

I SPY™

I SPY, You SPY, Let's all play I SPY!

SEARCH!

New I SPY video games include Ultimate I SPY for Wii™. A revolutionary way to play I SPY!

ESRB Rating: E for Everyone

PLAY!

New puzzles and games from  including I SPY Ready Set Silhouette and I SPY Flip 5!

WATCH!

Airs daily on

HBO Family®

For more I SPY Fun, log onto
www.scholastic.com/ISPY